Marvin's Trip to Mars

Written by
Laura Appleton-Smith

Illustrated by
Keinyo White

Laura Appleton-Smith holds a degree in English from Middlebury College.
Laura is a primary school teacher who has combined her talents in creative writing with
her experience in early childhood education to create *Books to Remember*.
She lives in New Hampshire with her husband, Terry.

Keinyo White is a graduate of the Rhode Island School of Design with a B.F.A. in illustration.
He currently produces children's books and freelance illustrations from his studio
in Los Angeles. This is his second book from Flyleaf Publishing.

A Book to Remember™
Published by Flyleaf Publishing

For orders or information, contact us at **(800) 449-7006**.
Please visit our website at **www.flyleafpublishing.com**

Fifth Edition 9/16
Library of Congress Catalog Card Number: 2001116541
Softcover ISBN-13: 978-1-929262-04-5
Printed and bound in the USA at Worzalla Publishing, Stevens Point, WI

For Terry

LAS

For Kari and Ajani

KW

"Hop up, Marvin. You can bring your rocket to bed," Mom tells Marvin as she pulls back his quilt.

2

"When I am big I will blast off in a rocket.
I will visit the planets and stars,"
Marvin tells Mom as she tucks him into bed.

4

"But for now, you can visit the planets and stars
in your imagination,"
Mom tells Marvin as she kisses him.

Mom pats Max the dog and clicks off the light.

It is dark.

Mars

10

Just then a red man with lots of arms
is standing next to Marvin's bed.

12

"I am Zar from Mars. I will do you no harm.
Do you want to visit Mars and the rest of the
planets and stars?"

"Yes, but I should ask Mom and Dad," Marvin tells him.

Mom and Dad are tucked in bed.

"Can I visit Mars?" Marvin asks.

"Yes Marvin, when you are big," Dad tells him.

"In your imagination, Marvin," Mom tells him.

16

Zar's rocket is parked in the back yard.

It hums and hisses and sparks.

Marvin straps into a harness.

Zar presses lots of buttons in the cockpit with his arms.

"5, 4, 3, 2, 1 — lift-off!"

The rocket blasts up and up—
so far that cars and trucks are just specks of light.

Marvin's yard is just a mark on the big planet Earth.

"Put on your dark glasses," Zar tells Marvin and Max.
"Next we will pass the sun."

The sun is so hot.

It is hard for Marvin to imagine that the rocket will not melt.

25

Past the sun Zar stops the rocket.
They drift in between the stars and planets.

"This is fantastic," Marvin tells Zar.
Max barks.

Zar hands Marvin a map.

"That distant red planet is Mars.
We can visit Mars and fill the rocket up with gas."

28

30

On Mars, Marvin begins to miss planet Earth.
He misses his Mom and Dad and his yard.

"Can we go back?" Marvin asks.
"Yes, as fast as you can imagine," Zar tells him.

As fast as that, Marvin is back in bed.
His rocket is in his arms.

Max is on the bed next to him.

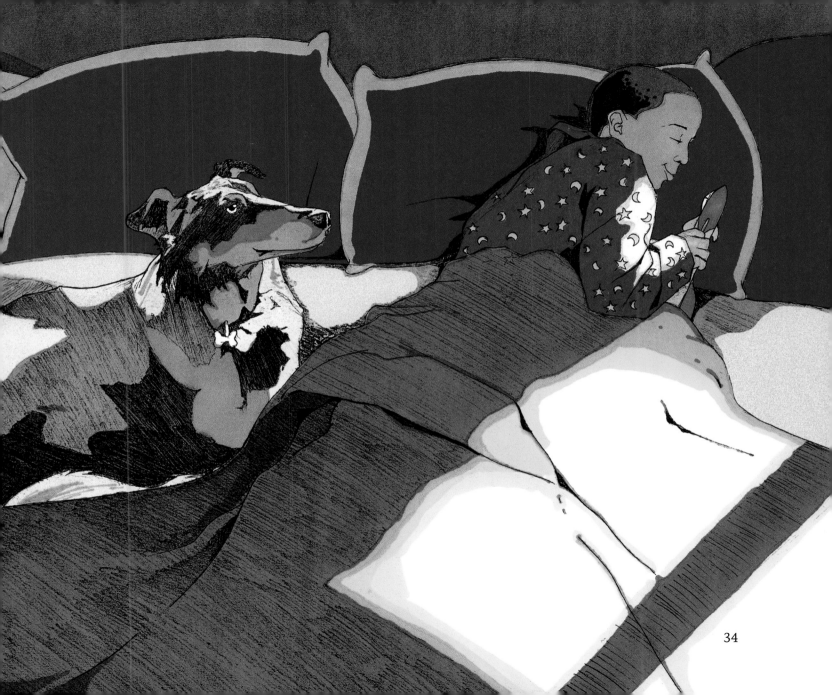

The sun was up.

Zar had departed.

There was no rocket in the yard.

Had Marvin and Max visited Mars,
or was Zar just part of Marvin's fantastic imagination?

It is up to you to decide…

Prerequisite Skills

Single consonants and short vowels
Final double consonants *ff*, *gg*, *ll*, *nn*, *ss*, *tt*, *zz*
Consonant /k/ *ck*
Consonant digraphs /ng/ *ng*, *n[k]*, /th/ *th*, /hw/ *wh*
Schwa /ə/ *a*, *e*, *i*, *o*, *u*
Long /ē/ *ee*, *y*
r-Controlled /ûr/ *er*
Variant vowel /aw/ *al*, *all*
Consonant /l/ *le*
/d/ or /t/ *–ed*

Prerequisite Skills are foundational phonics skills that have been previously introduced.

Target Letter-Sound Correspondence is the letter-sound correspondence introduced in the story.

High-Frequency Puzzle Words are high-frequency irregular words.

Story Puzzle Words are irregular words that are not high frequency.

Decodable Words are words that can be decoded solely on the basis of the letter-sound correspondences or phonetic elements that have been introduced.

Target Letter-Sound Correspondence

r-Controlled /ar/ sound spelled *ar*

arms	Marvin
barks	Marvin's
cars	parked
dark	part
far	sparks
hard	stars
harm	yard
harness	Zar
mark	Zar's
Mars	

High-Frequency Puzzle Words

are	pulls
between	put
do	she
for	should
from	so
go	there
he	they
into	to
light	want
no	was
now	we
of	you
or	your

Story Puzzle Words

begins	Earth
decide	imagination
departed	imagine

Decodable Words

1	blasts	glasses	lift-off	planet	then
2	bring	had	lots	planets	this
3	but	hands	man	presses	trip
4	buttons	him	map	quilt	trucks
5	can	his	Max	red	tucked
a	clicks	hisses	melt	rest	tucks
am	cockpit	hop	miss	rocket	up
and	Dad	hot	misses	specks	visit
as	distant	hums	Mom	standing	visited
ask	dog	I	next	stops	when
asks	drift	in	not	straps	will
back	fantastic	is	on	sun	with
bed	fast	it	pass	tells	yes
big	fill	just	past	that	
blast	gas	kisses	pats	the	